W9-BDN-883

Dear Parent:

Congratulations! Your child is taking the first steps on an exciting journey. The destination? Independent reading!

STEP INTO READING® will help your child get there. The program offers five steps to reading success. Each step includes fun stories and colorful art. There are also Step into Reading Sticker Books, Step into Reading Math Readers, Step into Reading Phonics Readers, Step into Reading Write-In Readers, and Step into Reading Phonics Boxed Sets—a complete literacy program with something to interest every child.

Learning to Read, Step by Step!

Ready to Read **Preschool–Kindergarten**
- big type and easy words • rhyme and rhythm • picture clues

For children who know the alphabet and are eager to begin reading.

Reading with Help **Preschool–Grade 1**
- basic vocabulary • short sentences • simple stories

For children who recognize familiar words and sound out new words with help.

Reading on Your Own **Grades 1–3**
- engaging characters • easy-to-follow plots • popular topics

For children who are ready to read on their own.

Reading Paragraphs **Grades 2–3**
- challenging vocabulary • short paragraphs • exciting stories

For newly independent readers who read simple sentences with confidence.

Ready for Chapters **Grades 2–4**
- chapters • longer paragraphs • full-color art

For children who want to take the plunge into chapter books but still like colorful pictures.

STEP INTO READING® is designed to give every child a successful reading experience. The grade levels are only guides. Children can progress through the steps at their own speed, developing confidence in their reading, no matter what their grade.

Remember, a lifetime love of reading starts with a single step!

Special thanks to Vicki Jaeger, Monica Okazaki, Ann McNeill, Emily Kelly,
Sharon Woloszyk, Julia Phelps, Tanya Mann, Rob Hudnut, Tiffany J. Shuttleworth,
Gabrielle Miles, M. Elizabeth Hughes, Lily Martinez, and Walter P. Martishius

BARBIE and associated trademarks and trade dress are owned by, and used under license from, Mattel, Inc.
Copyright © 2011 Mattel, Inc. All Rights Reserved.
Published in the United States by Random House Children's Books, a division of Random House, Inc., 1745 Broadway, New York, NY 10019, and in Canada by Random House of Canada Limited, Toronto.

Step into Reading, Random House, and the Random House colophon are registered trademarks of Random House, Inc.

Visit us on the Web!
StepIntoReading.com
www.randomhouse.com/kids
www.barbie.com

Educators and librarians, for a variety of teaching tools, visit us at
www.randomhouse.com/teachers

ISBN: 978-0-375-86932-7 (trade) — ISBN: 978-0-375-96932-4 (lib. bdg.)
Printed in the United States of America 10 9 8 7 6 5 4 3 2 1

Random House Children's Books supports the First Amendment and celebrates the right to read.

Adapted by Christy Webster
Based on the screenplay by Elise Allen
Illustrated by Das Grüp Incorporated

Random House New York

It is almost Christmas!
Barbie and her sisters
are going
to New York City.
They pack their bags.

The sisters are
on the plane.

It starts snowing!
The plane must land
in a small town.

Barbie takes her sisters to an inn.

The owner
loves Christmas!
The inn has
a Christmas tree
and presents.

Skipper loves music.

She sings.

Barbie hears her.

Skipper sounds great!

The next day,
it is still snowing.
The girls hang
stockings.
They will spend
Christmas at the inn.

XOXO

The sisters play
in the snow.
Chelsea meets a puppy!
His name is Rudy.
Rudy takes Chelsea
for a sled ride.

The girls find a barn.
They see reindeer!

Chelsea is excited.

She runs in.

The barn is full
of presents!
Chelsea thinks
it is Santa's barn!

The girls go back
to the inn.
Skipper sees a band.

They sound good!
She has an idea.
She will plan
a Christmas Eve concert!

Barbie wants
to help Skipper.

But Skipper wants
to plan the concert
by herself.
The girls fight.

Chelsea is upset.
She runs away
with Rudy.

Barbie, Skipper,
and Stacie look
for Chelsea.

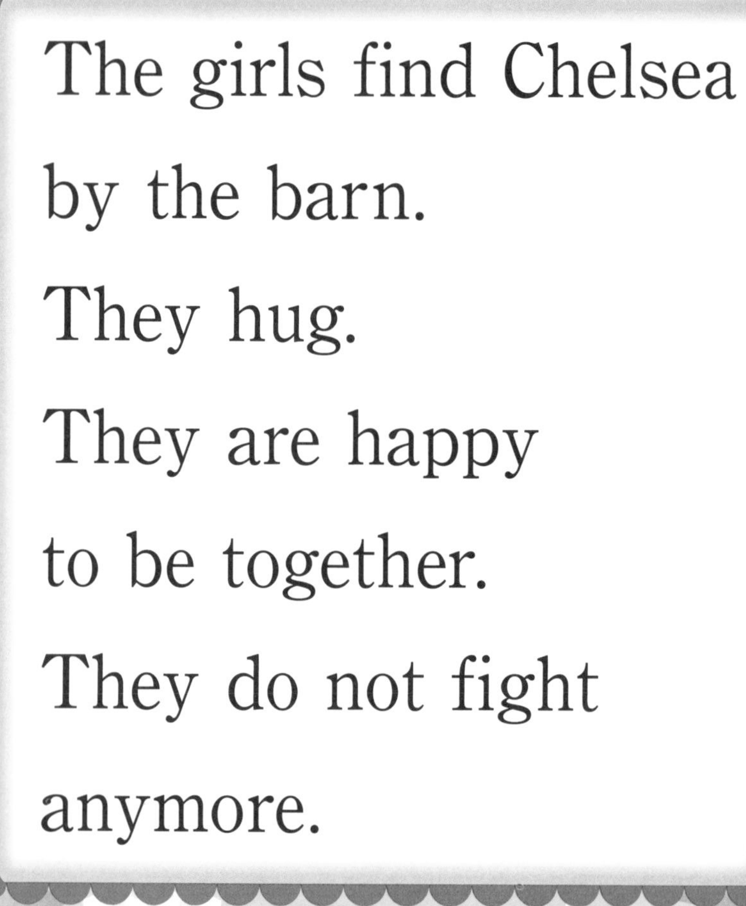

The girls find Chelsea
by the barn.
They hug.
They are happy
to be together.
They do not fight
anymore.

The sisters go
inside the barn.
The presents are gone!
Now there is a stage
with pretty lights.

Chelsea says Santa
put them up.
Skipper can
have her concert!

The sisters
work together.
They sing.
The band plays.

Rudy jumps.
The crowd dances.
The concert is great!

Barbie and her sisters have a perfect Christmas!